GW01607869

A Handful of Flowers

Compiled and illustrated by
Yvonne Skargon

ADAM & CHARLES BLACK
LONDON

First published 1980
A & C Black (Publishers) Ltd
35 Bedford Row, London WC1R 4JH

Compiled and illustrated
with original wood engravings
by Yvonne Skargon

ISBN 0 7136 2049 8

A handful of flowers.—(Present day books).
1. Wild flowers—Literary collections
2. English literature
3. Skargon, Yvonne
4. Wild flowers in art
I. Skargon, Yvonne   II. Series
820′.8′036   PR1111.W/

ISBN 0-7136-2049-8

Typeset by Santype International Ltd.,
Salisbury, Wilts
Printed in Great Britain by Cedar Colour Ltd

The showre of Blossomes

Love in a showre of Blossomes came
Down, and halfe drown'd me with the same:
The Blooms that fell were white and red;
But with such sweets commingled,
As whether (this) I cannot tell
My sight was pleas'd more, or my smell:
But true it was, as I rowl'd there,
Without a thought of hurt, or feare;
Love turn'd himselfe into a Bee,
And with his Javelin wounded me:
From which mishap this use I make,
Where most sweets are, there lyes a Snake.
Kisses and Favours are sweet things;
But Those have thorns, and These have stings.

ROBERT HERRICK

CHRISTMAS ROSE

Then may you shoulder spade and hoe,
And heavy booted homeward go
For no new flowers shall be born
Save Hellebore on Christmas morn.
VITA SACKVILLE WEST

The last and first flower of the year. The word hellebore comes from the Greek helein, to kill, and bora, food. It is said to be poisonous, but baleful as the aura of the hellebore may seem the plant was always allowed some good qualities too. Legend tells how one, Mecampe, a cowherd, discovered that hellebores acted as a healthy purgative on his cattle. With this useful knowledge he set up and became a physician, and soon became famous. Proetus, King of Argos, called him in to cure the madness of his daughters who were under the delusion that they had been changed into cows. Fortunately the treatment succeeded, and the hand of one of the princesses was given in marriage to Mecampe as a reward. As a result of this an alternative name for hellebore was mecampodium, to acknowledge its good qualities as well as its bad ones.

In addition to guarding the homestead from ill the hellebore was regarded as a wonderful antidote against madness, and such is spoken of by Burton, who introduces it among the emblems of his frontispiece, in his *Anatomie of Melancholy*.

'Borage and hellebore fill two scenes,
Sovereign plants to purge the veins
Of melancholy, and cheer the heart
Of those black fumes which make it smart;
To clear the brain of misty fogs,
Which dull our senses and soul clogs;
The best medicine that e'er God made
For this malady, if well assay'd.

But it has been observed, our forefathers, in strewing their floors with this plant, were introducing a real evil into their houses, instead of an imaginary one, the perfume having been considered highly pernicious to health.

Hellebore was not only considered a certain antidote against madness but also a plant of ill omen.

By the witches tower,
Where hellebore and hemlock seem to weave
Round its dark vaults a melancholy bower
For spirits of the dead at night's enchanted hour.
THOMAS CAMPBELL

The Christmas rose, the last flower of the year,
Comes when the holly-berries glow and cheer,
When the pale snowdrop rises from the earth,
So white and spirit-like 'mid Christmas mirth.

There are three sorts of blacke Hellebor or Beares Foote, one that is the true and right kind, whose flowers have the most beautiful aspect, and in the time of his flowering most rare, that is, in the deepe of winter, about Christmas, when no other can be seen upon the ground . . . We call it in English, the true blacke Hellebor, or the Christmas flower.
JOHN PARKINSON

SNOWDROP

From hidden bulb the flower reared up
Its angled, slender, cold, dark stem,
Whence dangled an inverted cup
    For tri-leaved diadem.

Beneath these ice-pure sepals lay
A triplet of green-pencilled snow,
Which in the chill-aired gloom of day
    Stirred softly to and fro.

WALTER DE LA MARE

An angel was sent to console Eve when she was mourning over the barren earth. Now, no flower grew in Eden, and the driving snow kept falling to form a pall for earth's untimely funeral after the fall of man. But as the angel spoke, he caught a flake of falling snow, breathed on it, and bade it take form, and bud and blow. Ere it reached the ground it had turned into a beautiful flower, which Eve prized more than all the other fair plants in Paradise; for the angel said to her

> 'This in an earnest, Eve, to thee,
> That sun and summer soon shall be.'

The angel's mission ended, he departed, but where he had stood a ring of snowdrops formed a lovely posy.

February 14th, Sunday. A fine morning. The sun shines but it has been a hard frost in the night. There are some little snowdrops that are afraid to pop their white heads quite out, and a few blossoms of hepatica that are half-starved.
DOROTHY WORDSWORTH

A snowdrop was to me, as to Wordsworth, part of the Sermon on the Mount; but I never should have written sonnets to the celandine, because it is of a coarse yellow, and imperfect form.
JOHN RUSKIN

Odd hive bees fancying winter oer
And dreaming in their combs of spring
Creeps on the slab beside the door
And strokes its legs upon its wing
While wild ones half asleep are humming
Round snowdrop bells a feeble note
And pigions coo of summer coming
Picking their feathers on the cote
JOHN CLARE

As Flora's breath, by some transforming power,
Had changed an icicle into a flower.
MRS BARBAULD

Like pendant flakes of vegetating snow,
  The early herald of the infant year,
Ere yet the adventurous crocus dares to blow,
  Beneath the orchard boughs thy buds appear.

While still the cold north-east ingenial lowers,
  And scarce the hazel in the leafless copse
Or shallows show their downy powdered flowers,
  The grass is spangled with thy silver drops.

Yet when those pallid blossoms shall give place
  To countless tribes of richer hue and scent,
Summer's gay blooms, and Autumn's yellow race,
  I shall thy pale inodorous bells lament.
CHARLOTTE SMITH

DAFFODIL

Daffodils,
That come before the swallow dares,
and take
The winds of March with beauty.
WILLIAM SHAKESPEARE

To Daffadilies

Faire Daffadills, we weep to see
You haste away so soone:
As yet the early-rising Sun
Has not attain'd his Noone.
Stay, stay,
Until the hasting day
Has run
But to the Even-song;
And, having pray'd together, we
Will goe with you along.

We have short time to stay, as you,
We have as short a Spring;
As quick a growth to meet Decay,
As you, or any thing.
We die,
As your hours doe, and drie
Away,
Like to the Summers raine;
Or as the pearles of Mornings dew
Ne'r to be found againe

ROBERT HERRICK

See that there be stores of lilies,
Called by shepherds daffodillies.

MICHAEL DRAYTON

The Daffodil was regarded by early writers as a member of the lily family, and it has even been conjectured that its name is nothing but a corruption of Dis's lily, as it is supposed to be the flower that dropped from Pluto's chariot when he was carrying off Proserpine to the infernal regions.

She stepped upon Sicilian grass,
  Demeter's daughter fresh and fair,
A child of light, a radiant lass,
  And gamesome as the morning air.
The daffodils were fair to see,
They nodded lightly on the lea.

Lo! one she marked of rarer growth
  Than orchis or anemone;
For it the maiden left them both,
  And parted from her company.
Drawn nigh, she deemed it fairer still,
And stooped to gather by the rill
The daffodil, the daffodil.

What ailed the meadow that it shook?
  What ailed the air of Sicily?
She wandered by the brattling brook,
  And trembled with the trembling lea.
'The coal-black horses rise—they rise:
O mother, mother!' low she cries.

'O light, light!' she cries, 'farewell;
The coal-black horses wait for me.
O shade of shades, where I must dwell,
Demeter, mother, far from thee!
Oh, fated doom that I fulfil!
Oh, fateful flower beside the rill!
The daffodil, the daffodil!'
JEAN INGELOW

Divination by a Daffadill

When a Daffadill I see,
Hanging down his head t'wards me;
Guesse I may, what I must be:
First, I shall decline my head;
Secondly, I shall be dead;
Lastly, safely buryed.
ROBERT HERRICK

When daffodils begin to peer,
With heigh! the doxy over the dale,
Why, then comes in the sweet o' the year.
WILLIAM SHAKESPEARE

FORGET-ME-NOT

The sweet forget-me-nots,
That grow for happy lovers.
ALFRED LORD TENNYSON

A knight and his betrothed were walking on the banks of a river, when the lady espied a bunch of the *Myosotris palustris* (as the blossom is termed by Linnaeus) floating down the stream; and expressing a wish to possess it, with chivalrous promptitude the mail-clad gallant plunged into the river and grasped the flower; but, alas! encumbered by the weight of his armour, he was unable to remount the slippery bank. Finding himself, despite all his exertions, sinking fast beneath the waters, with a last effort he flung the blossoms ashore to his agonized mistress, crying, ere he sank for ever, 'Forget me not!'

Another event connected with chivalry, other than the melancholy one from which it takes its name. When Lord Scales, brother to Elizabeth Woodville, wife of Edward IV, tilted against a French knight of Burgundy, the ladies of the Court playfully presented him with a collar of gold, brilliantly enamelled with these little blossoms, as a fitting reward for an English knight's emprise of arms either on horseback or on foot. This incident shows the admiration in which this simple wild flower has been held for a long time.

A legend told by the poet Shiraz, respecting the origin of the forget-me-not. 'It was in the golden morning of the early world, when an angel sat weeping outside the closed gates of Eden. He had fallen from his high estate through loving a daughter of earth, nor was he permitted to enter again until she whom he loved had planted the flowers of the forget-me-not in every corner of the world. He returned to earth and assisted her, and they went hand in hand over the world planting the forget-me-not. When their task was ended, they entered Paradise together; for the fair woman, without tasting the bitterness of death, became immortal like the angel, whose love her beauty had won, when she sat by the river twining the forget-me-not in her hair.'

> That blue and bright-eyed flowret of the brook
> Hope's gentle gem, the sweet forget-me-not!

TULIP

The later Herbarists by a Turkish or strange name call it Tulipa, of the Dalmatian cap called Tulipa, 'the forme whereof the floure when it is open seemeth to represent.' It is called in English after the Turkish name Tulipa, or it may be called Dalmation Cap, or the Turks Cap. What name the antient Writers gave it is not certainly knowne.

I do verily thinke that these are the Lillies of the field mentioned by our Saviour, Mat. 6.28,29, for he saith, That Solomon in all his royaltie was not arrayed like one of these. The reasons that induce me to thinke thus, are these; First, their shape: for their floures resemble Lillies; and in these places whereas our Saviour was conversant they grow wilde in the fields. Secondly, the infinite varietie of colour, which is to be found more in this than any other sort of floure. And thirdly, the wondrous beautie and mixtures of these floures. This is my opinion, and these my reasons, which any may either approve of or gainsay, as he shall thinke good.

JOHN GERARD

Its original home is presumed to be Persia, and its name is considered a corruption of the Persian word for turban, to which article of attire it bears a similarity. In the middle of the sixteenth century, Busbeck, the Emperor of Germany's ambassador to the Sultan, was attracted by the gay colours of this flower, and on his return to his native land, took some of the bulbs back with him. They soon became great favourites, and were imported into Italy, England, France and before long into every European climate. In Holland all classes were infected with an extraordinary desire to possess rare specimens of the tulip: not necessarily for love of the flower, but rather with a view to participate in the pecuniary speculations to which it gave rise. Large amounts of money changed hands to possess a root of a peculiar species. A connoisseur possessing a very magnificent specimen, heard that there existed one of a similar kind at Haarlem. He journeyed to that city, purchased the rival blossom at an enormous outlay, and as soon as it became his, crushed it to pulp with his foot, crying out in ecstacy, 'Now my tulip is unique!'

Other more ludicrous stories are related to this curious mental epidemic; one tale runs that while the mania was at its height, a sailor, going into a merchant's counting-house, saw a bulb which he mistook for an onion; he popped it into his pocket, and took it off to aid him in relishing a red herring which he had got for dinner. The merchant missing the bulb, which was that of a high-priced tulip, suspected the sailor, rushed after him, and caught him—finishing his meal off the ill-flavoured onion! The sailor, who for once had dined like a prince, expiated his mistake by six month's imprisonment.

. . . then comes the tulip race, where beauty plays
Her idle freaks: from family diffused
To family, as flies the father dust
The varied colours run: and while they break
On the charmed eye, the exulting Florist marks
With secret pride, the wonders of his hand.
JAMES THOMSON

So cosmopolitan, these English tulips,
To cottager as native as himself!
Aliens, that Shakespeare neither saw nor sang.
Alien Asiatics, that have blown
Between the boulders of a Persian hill
Long centuries before they reached the dykes
To charm Van Huysum and the curious Breughel,
And Rachel Ruysch, so nice so leisurely
That seven years were given to two pictures.
VITA SACKVILLE WEST

COLUMBINE

May 28th, Friday 1802. The sky cloudy, the air sweet and cool. The young bull finches, in their party-coloured raiment, bustle about among the blossoms, and poize themselves like wire-dancers or tumblers, shaking the twigs and dashing off the blossoms. There is yet one primrose in the orchard. The stitchwort is fading. The wild columbines are coming into beauty, the vetches are in abundance, blossoming and seeding. That pretty little wavy-looking dial-like yellow flower, the speedwell, and some others, whose names I do not yet know. The wild columbines are coming into beauty—some of the gowans fading.

DOROTHY WORDSWORTH

Why, when so many fairer shine,
Why choose the homely colombine?
Tis Folly's flower, that homely one,
        That universal guest,
Makes every garden but a type
        Of every human breast;
For though ye tend both mind and bower,
There's still a nook for Folly's flower.

LOUISA TWAMLEY

The shining pansy, trimmed with golden lace;
The tall topped lark-heels, feathered thick with
  flowers;
The woodbine, climbing o'er the door in bowers;
The London tufts of many a mottled hue;
The pale pink pea, and monkshood darkly blue;
The white and purple gillyflowers, that stay
Lingering in blossom summer half away;
The single blood walls, of a luscious smell,
Old-fashioned flowers which housewives love so well;
The columbines, stone blue, or deep night brown,
Their honey-comb like blossoms hanging down;
Each cottage garden's fond adopted child,
Though heaths still claim them, where they yet
  grow wild;
With marjoram knots, sweet brier, and ribbon grass,
And lavender, the choice of every lass.

JOHN CLARE

CARNATIONS

The curious choice clove July flower,
  Whose kinds, hight the carnation,
For sweetness of most sovereign power
  Shall help my wreath to fashion;
Whose sundry colours of one kind,
  First from one root derived,
Them in their several suits I'll bind,
  My garland so contrived.

MICHAEL DRAYTON

The gillyflower is in old ballads, one of the flowers thought to grow in paradise.

The fields about this city faire
  Were all with roses set,
Gillyflowers and carnations faire,
  Which canker could not fret.

The carnation was popular in France as well as in England and it is said the famous soldier the Great Conde, who was incarcerated in the Bastille at the time of Fronde grew carnations to lighten the long hours of captivity.

Ther springen herbes, greet and smale,
The licorys and the cetewale,
  And many a clow gilofre;
And notemuge to put in ale,
Whethir it be moist or stale,
  Or for to lay in cofre.

GEOFFREY CHAUCER

Carnations if you look close have their tongue-shaped petals powdered with spankled red glister, which no doubt gives them their brilliancy: sharp chip shadows of one petal on another: the notched edge curls up and so is darked, which gives them graceful precision.

GERARD MANLEY HOPKINS

Clove Gillofloures There are at this day under the name of Cariophyllus comprehended divers and sundry sorts of plants, of such various colours, and also several shapes, that a great and large volume would not suffice to write of every one at large in particular; considering how infinite they are, and how every year clymate and country bringeth forth new sorts, such as have not heretofore been written of; some whereof are called Carnations, others Clove Gillofloures, some Sops in wine, some Pagiants, or Paigion color, Horse-flesh, blunket, purple, white, double and single gillofloures. . . .

The conserve made of the floures of the Clove Gillofloure and sugar, is exceeding cordiall, and wonderfully above measure doth comfort the heart, being eaten now and then.
JOHN GERARD

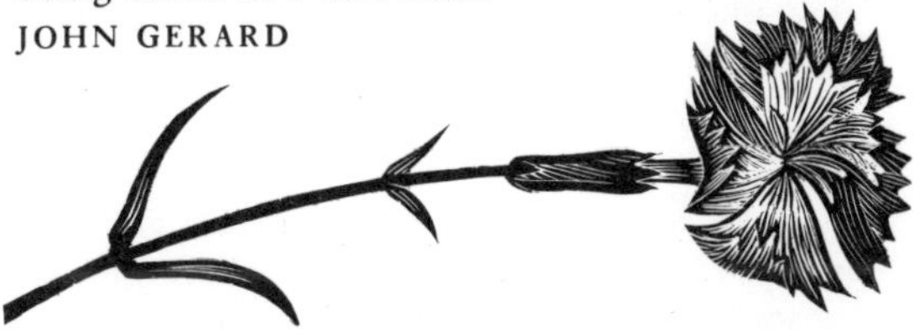

Sir, the year growing ancient,
Not yet on summer's death, nor on the birth
Of trembling winter, the fairest flowers o' the
  season
Are our carnations, and streak'd gillyvors.
WILLIAM SHAKESPEARE

MARIGOLD

The marigold, that goes to bed wi' the sun,
And with him rises, weeping.
WILLIAM SHAKESPEARE

Marygold, the classic name for this flower is Calendula, it is referred to as 'the flower of all months' in consequence of its blossoming the whole year—a statement scarcely borne out by facts so far as England is concerned. These plants are often called 'golds' by some English poets, the name of the Virgin Mary was a very frequent addition in the middle ages to anything useful or beautiful, and so in course of time the flower became known as the marygold.

When, with a serious musing, I behold
The grateful and obsequious marygold,
How duly every morning she displays
Her open breast when Phoebus spreads his rays;
How she observes him in her daily walk,
Still bending towards him her small slender stalk;
How, when he down declines, she droops and
mourns,
Bedew'd, as 't were, with tears till he returns;
And how she veils her flowers when he is gone,
As if she scorn'd to be looked upon
By an inferior eye, or did contemn
To wait upon a meaner light than him.
When this I meditate, methinks the flowers
Have spirits far more generous than ours,
And give us fair examples to despise
The servile fawnings and idolatries
Wherewith we court these earthly things below,
Which merit not the service we bestow.

GEORGE WITHER

Linnaeus has said that the marygold is usually open from nine in the morning till three in the afternoon; this foreshows a continuance of dry weather: should the blossom remain closed, rain may be expected. The circumstance, and the fact of its always turning its golden face towards the giver of day, has caused this plant to be sometimes termed 'the sun follower,' and the 'spouse of the sun.'

Open afresh your round of starry folds,
Ye ardent marigolds!
Dry up the moisture from your golden lids,
For great Apollo bids
That in these days your praises shall be sung
On many harps, which he has lately strung;
And when again your dewiness he kisses,
Tell him, I have you in my world of blisses:
So haply when I rove in some far vale,
His mighty voice may come upon the gale.
JOHN KEATS

The flower continues to bloom until stopped by the frost:
Coarse marygold, in days of yore I scorned thy tawny face,
But since my plants are frail and few, I've given thee welcome place.
MRS SIGOURNEY

The Marigold whose courtier's face
Echoes the Sun and doth unlace
Her at his rise, at his full stop
Packs and shuts up her gaudy shop.
JOHN CLEVELAND

The Marybudde, that shutteth with the light.
THOMAS CHATTERTON

ROSE

It is sometimes said that the red rose was originally white, but received a rosy hue from blood drawn by a thorn from the foot of Venus, as she was hastening to the aid of her adored Adonis. The ruddy tint has been ascribed to the kisses of Eve, and some to those of the Goddess of Love, from whose bath, Greek writers say, it originally sprang; whilst the full-bosomed cabbage rose, they say, sprang from the tears of Lycurgus, the enemy of Bacchus.

Numerous Persian poets have sung the praises of 'the blooming rose;' and from Jami we learn that the first rose appeared in Gulistan at the time the flowers demanded a new sovereign from Allah, because the drowsy lotus would slumber at night. At first the maiden queen was snowy white, and encircled with a protecting guard of thorns; but the poor nightingale fell into such an ecstasy of love over her charms, and so recklessly pressed his love-lorn and musical heart against those cruel thorns, that his blood, so far as it could trickle into the blossom's bosom, dyed it crimson; and, as the poet observes, 'are not the petals white at the extremity where the poor little birds's blood could not reach?'

The loves of the nightingale and the rose have many times been alluded to. This melodious bird appears in the East at the season when its adored flower begins to blow, which has engendered the poetical fiction that it bursts forth from its bud at the song of its admirer.

> Oh, sooner shall the rose of May
>   Mistake her own sweet nightingale,
> And to some meaner minstrel's lay
>   Open her bosom's glowing veil,
> Than love shall ever doubt a tone—
> A breath—of the beloved one!
>
> THOMAS MOORE

JAMI asserts with poetic freedom that 'You may place a handful of fragrant herbs and flowers before the nightingale; yet he wishes not in his constant heart for more than the sweet breath of his beloved rose.'

Though rich the spot
  With every flower this earth has got,
What is it to the nightingale
  If there his darling rose is not?

Once more see the nightingale, languid and faint,
Pours forth to the garden his sorrowful plaint:
May the rose ever flourish in beauty and bloom;
May evil ne'er touch her, misfortune ne'er come;
Long, long may she flourish wherever she's seen,
And rule 'midst the flowers as the sovereign
  queen!
But, oh, may she smile with less scornful an eye,
Nor leave her poor lovers to languish and die!

The rose, o'er crag or vale,
Sultana of the nightingale,
  The maid for whom his melody,
  His thousand songs, are heard on high,
Blooms blushing to her lover's tale:
His queen, the garden queen, his rose,
Unbent by winds, unchill'd by snows,
Far from the winters of the west,
By every breeze and season blest,
Returns the sweets by nature given
In softest incense back to heaven.

Thackeray gives his version of the legend:

Under the boughs I sat and listened still,
I could not have my fill.
'How comes' I said, 'such music to his bill?
Tell me for whom he sings so beautiful a trill.'

'Once I was dumb,' then did the bird disclose,
'But looked upon the rose,
And in the garden where the loved one grows,
I straightway did begin sweet music to compose.'

A prominent position is assigned to the Rose Garden of Worms: the fragile rampart that surrounded that famous garden was nothing more than a silken thread. Being attacked by giants, it was triumphantly defended by a band of knights, to each of whom Princess Chrymhild assigned a chaplet of roses and a kiss as a reward. It is said that one of the knights, named Hildebrandt, whilst accepting the chaplet, declined the salute; but that another, who was a monk named Ilsan, was so pleased with the proffered recompense that he begged for the bestowal of similar upon each of the fifty-two monks inhabiting the convent to which he belonged. His request was granted, but not until he had slain fifty-two of the gigantic offenders.

> 'Rosebud set with little wilful thorns,
> And sweet as English air could make her.'
> ALFRED LORD TENNYSON

The finest attar of roses comes from the East; it is the most exquisite of perfumes, and only obtained at great cost. The account of its first production is one of the legends of Oriental profusion. The Princess Nourmahal collected sufficient rosewater to fill a canal, on which was launched the boat that bore her, the Great Mogul, and all their attendants.

The extreme heat caused the rosewater to evaporate so rapidly that an oily substance spread over the surface of the canal. This was gathered up, and found to be a most delicious perfume, afterwards well known as the attar, or fragrant essence of rose.

See with what simplicity
This nymph begins her golden days!
In the green grass she loves to lie,
And there with her fair aspect tames
The wilder flowers, and gives them names:
But only with the roses plays;
            And them does tell
What colour best becomes them, and what smell.
ANDREW MARVELL

A rose, in water, to its stem
Decoys a myriad beads of air;
And, lovely with the light on them,
Gives even its thorns their share.
WALTER DE LA MARE

How the white rose became red

'As Cupid danced among
The gods, he down the nectar flung,
Which, on the white rose shed,
Made it for ever after red.'

Roses were more highly prized by the Romans than any other flower: they considered them emblematic of joy, and, in conformity with that idea, represented Comus, the God of Feasting, as a handsome young man, crowned with a garland of roses, whose leaves glistened with dew-drops. They were accustomed to strew their streets with roses at their chief festivals. Heliogabalus had his bed, apartments, and porticoes strewed with the rarest flowers; and, before him Cicero reproached Verres with having travelled through Sicily, seated on roses, with a crown of flowers on his head, and another round his neck.

Gulistan, so famed in Persian story, is the place where so many roses were grown that it was a five days' camel-ride through the great garden. Thence was brought the precious attar for the Shah's own use, and thence came daily fresh-plucked petals for the bed of the Sultana, who could not sleep if the rose-leaves were too much crumpled.

PANSY

There's pansies, that's for thoughts, pray you, love remember.
WILLIAM SHAKESPEARE

To Pansies

Ah, cruell Love! must I endure
Thy many scorns, and find no cure?
Say, are thy medicines made to be
Helps to all others, but to me?
Ile leave thee, and to Pansies come;
Comforts you'l afford me some:
You can ease my heart, and doe
What Love co'd ne'r be brought unto.
ROBERT HERRICK

Culpeper says, 'This is that herb which such physicians as are licensed to blaspheme by authority, without danger of having their tongues burned through with a hot iron, called an 'herb of the Trinity'.' 'It is also called by those that are more moderate,' he adds, 'Three-faces-in-a-hood;' 'love-in-idleness;' 'call-me-to-you;' and in Sussex we call them 'pancies'.'

Other writers had different methods of spelling this flower's name:

Now the shining meads
Do boast the paunse, lily, and the rose,
And every flower doth laugh as zephyr blows.
BEN JONSON

The humble little heart's-ease flower has not always known floral fame: in the year 1812, Lady Mary Bennett, then residing at Walton-on-Thames, had a great love for the flower and had a small garden planted entirely with it.

The gardener, wishing to please her, selected the seed of the choicest varieties, and to his pleasurable astonishment, on germinating, the seedlings displayed the most marvellous diversity of beauty and style. Milton's 'pansy freaked with jet' and even Shakespeare's purple 'love in idleness' were far outshone by these pampered children of Nature. Their breeder proudly displayed his triumphs to fellow-florists, and in a little while the heart's-ease ranked amongst the flowers of fashion.

And as proud as all of them
Bound in one, the garden's gem,
Heart's-ease, like a gallant bold,
In his cloth of purple and gold.
LEIGH HUNT

Yet mark'd I where the bolt of Cupid fell—
It fell upon a little western-flower,
Before milk-white, now purple with love's wound,
And maidens call it love-in-idleness.
WILLIAM SHAKESPEARE

The smaller varieties are scentless, some of the larger ones have a pleasant perfume—scarcely so powerful as the following poem would suggest:

The pansy and the violet here,
  As seeming to descend
Both from one root, a very pair,
  For sweetness do contend.

And pointing to a pink to tell
  Which bears it, it is loth
To judge it, but replies, for smell,
  That it excels them both.

Wherewith displeased they hang their heads,
  So angry soon they grow,
And from their odoriferous beds
  Their sweets at it they throw.

MICHAEL DRAYTON

Pansies to please the sight, and cassia sweet to smell,

JOHN DRYDEN

LAVENDER

Here's flowers for you;
Hot lavender, mints, savory, marjoram.
WILLIAM SHAKESPEARE

By the Greeks the name Nardus is given to Lavender, from Naarda, a city of Syria near the Euphrates, and many persons call the plant Nard. St. Mark mentions this as Spikenard, a thing of great value. . . In Pliny's time, blossoms of the Nardus sold for a hundred Roman denarii (or £3 2s 6d) the pound. This Lavender or Nardus was called Asarum by the Romans, because it was not used in garlands or chaplets. It was formerly believed that the asp, a dangerous kind of viper, made Lavender its habitual place of abode, so that the plant had to be approached with great caution.

Mercury owns this herb. It is of especial use in pains of the head and brain which proceed from cold, apoplexy, falling-sickness, the dropsy, or sluggish malady, cramps, convolsions, palsies, and often faintings.
NICHOLAS CULPEPER

The distilled water of Lavander smelt unto, or the temples and forehead bathed therewith, is refreshing to them that have Catalepsy, a light migram, and to them that have the falling sicknesse, and that use to swoune much. . .
The floures of Lavander picked from the knaps, I meane the blew part and not the husk, mixed with Cinnamon, Nutmegs, & Cloves, made into pouder, and given to drinke in the distilled water thereof, doth helpe the panting and passion of the heart, prevaileth against giddinesse, turning, or swimming of the braine, and members subject to palsie.

JOHN GERARD

Lavender, whose spikes of azure bloom
Shall be, erewhile, in arid bundles bound,
To lurk amidst the labours of her loom,
And crown her kerchiefs clean with mickle rare
  perfume.

WILLIAM SHENSTONE

Out of Time? Out of Tune

We blame, nay we despise her paines
That wets her Garden when it raines:
But when the drought has dri'd the knot;
Then let her use the watring pot.
We pray for showers (at our need)
To drench, but not to drown our seed.

ROBERT HERRICK

ACKNOWLEDGEMENTS

Extracts from the writings of Walter de la Mare reproduced by permission of the Literary Trustees of Walter de la Mare and the Society of Authors as their representative.

Extracts from the writings of Vita Sackville West reproduced by permission of Nigel Nicolson and Curtis Brown Ltd.

Extracts from the writings of John Clare reproduced by permission of Eric Robinson and Curtis Brown Ltd.